A BOOK of LOVE

by Emma Randall

Penguin Workshop

Love is something we all need,
every single day.

It really isn't hard to show,
and give in your own way.

We often show our love with touch,
like a great big hug or kiss.

But there are lots of ways to show you care,
and ideas not to miss.

If Grandpa needs a
helping hand,

or Grannie walks
quite slow,

being patient
shows your love.
Just wait and
watch it grow.

FLAVORS
Vanilla
Strawberry
Chocolate
Mint Chocchip

Ice Cream

If somebody is feeling down,

or having a rotten day,

simply listening is enough
to help make things okay.

Thoughtful presents show your love,
I hope you are aware.

Making someone feel special
lets them know you care.

Love is shown through
kind acts, too,
like washing dirty dishes.

Or you could bring Mom a piece of cake
with candles for birthday wishes!

To offer a gentle word or two,
and consider how others feel,
are both examples of selfless acts
that prove your love is real.

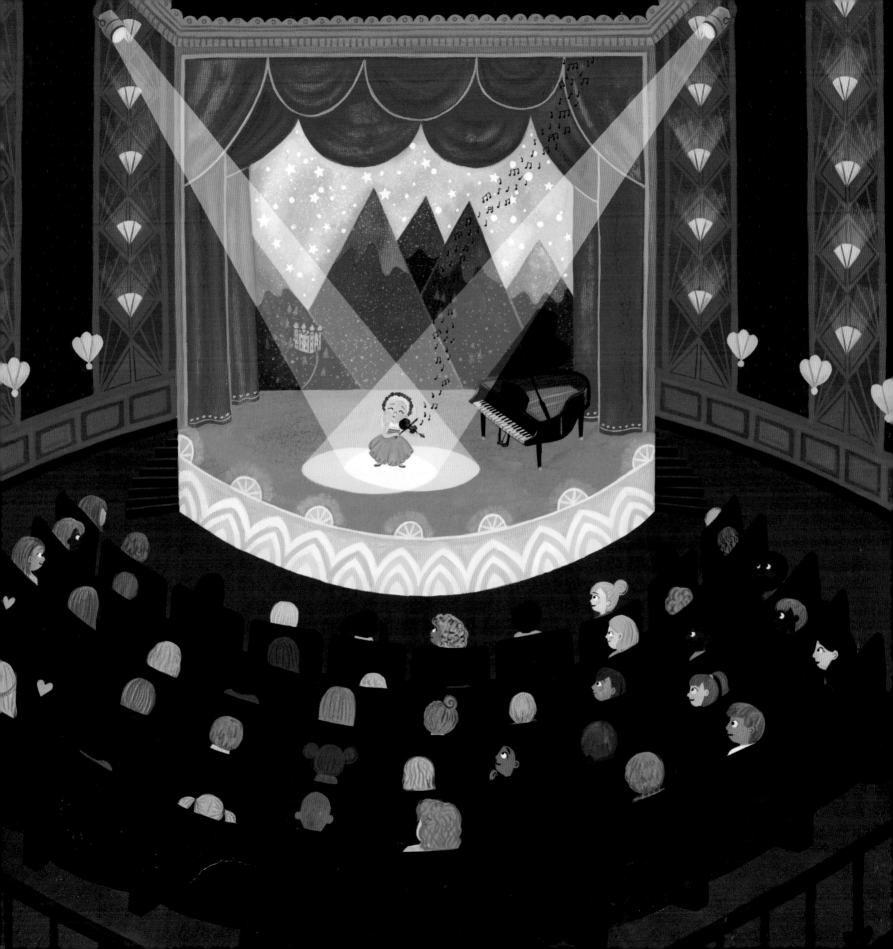

Sometimes loving can be hard,
when someone makes us blue.

But forgiving and forgetting helps
and is the right thing to do.

When your sister sneaks into your room,
taking toys when you're not there,

you could get mad
and stamp your feet,
but it's loving to
let her share.

If somebody is feeling small, or even needs protection,

show support, stand up for them,
and offer some affection.

It's hard sometimes to
see the good in people
who aren't kind.

But if you can, look past their faults.

It's surprising what you might find.

We're all wonderfully different,
and come in many colors and sizes.

If we love each other as we are,
just watch how everyone rises.

Everyone on earth needs love,
this gift we give for free.

And if we all loved one another like this,
think how lovely the world would be!

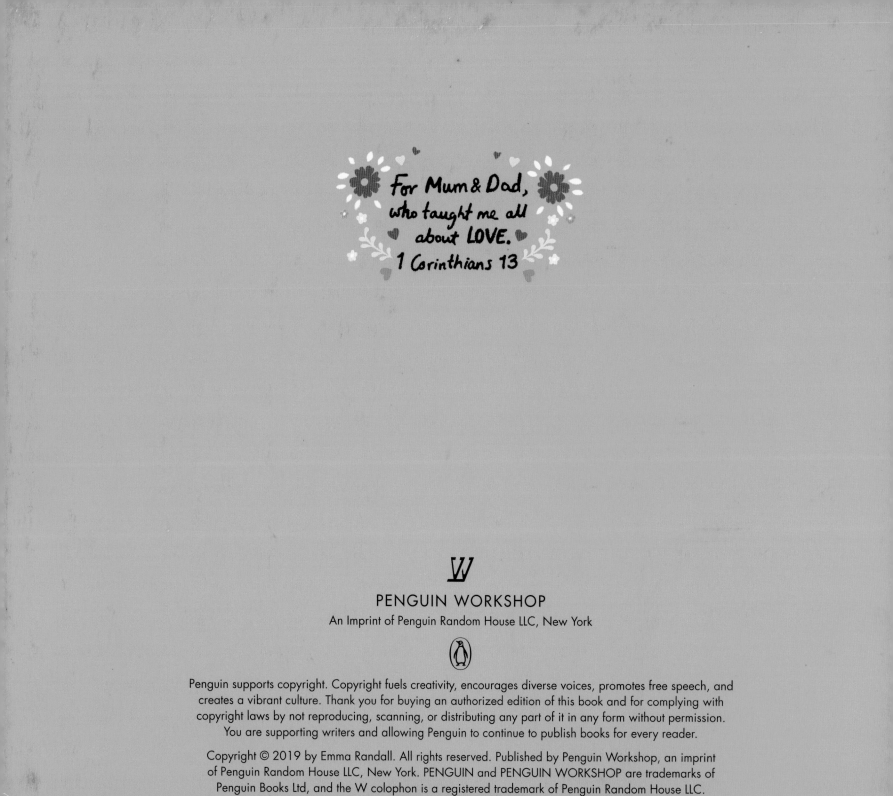

For Mum & Dad,
who taught me all
about LOVE.
1 Corinthians 13

PENGUIN WORKSHOP

An Imprint of Penguin Random House LLC, New York

Penguin supports copyright. Copyright fuels creativity, encourages diverse voices, promotes free speech, and creates a vibrant culture. Thank you for buying an authorized edition of this book and for complying with copyright laws by not reproducing, scanning, or distributing any part of it in any form without permission. You are supporting writers and allowing Penguin to continue to publish books for every reader.

Copyright © 2019 by Emma Randall. All rights reserved. Published by Penguin Workshop, an imprint of Penguin Random House LLC, New York. PENGUIN and PENGUIN WORKSHOP are trademarks of Penguin Books Ltd, and the W colophon is a registered trademark of Penguin Random House LLC. Manufactured in China.

Visit us online at www.penguinrandomhouse.com.

Library of Congress Cataloging-in-Publication Data is available upon request.

ISBN 9781524793319   10 9 8 7 6 5 4 3 2 1